GUS

A BEAVER

by Bonnie Highsmith Taylor

Perfection Learning®

Dedication

For Linda D. Williams

About the Author

Bonnie Highsmith Taylor is a native Oregonian. She loves camping in the Oregon mountains and watching birds and other wildlife. Writing is Ms. Taylor's first love. But she also enjoys going to plays and concerts, collecting antique dolls, and listening to good music.

Ms. Taylor is the author of several Animal Adventures books, including *Kip: A Sea Otter* and *Roscoe: A North American Moose.*

Cover Photo: Windland Rice

Image Credits: Tom and Pat Leeson pp. 12, 14–15, 16, 18, 20, 22, 26, 30, 33, 38 (photo)

ArtToday (some images copyright www.arttoday.com); Corel Professional Photos pp. 10, 23, 28, 36, 48, 50, 54; Corel.com pp. 5, 25, 40, 42–43, 44–45, 46–47, 49

Printed in the United States of America. For information, contact
Perfection Learning® Corporation, 1000 North Second Avenue,
P.O. Box 500, Logan, Iowa 51546-0500.
Tel: 1-800-831-4190 • Fax: 1-712-644-2392
Paperback ISBN 0-7891-5262-2
Cover Craft® ISBN 0-7807-9663-2
2 3 4 5 6 7 PP 10 09 08 07 06 05

CONTENTS

Chapter 1 6

Chapter 2 13

Chapter 3 21

Chapter 4 25

Chapter 5 34

Chapter 6 41

CHAPTER

It was late spring. Two young beavers swam up a small stream. They were looking for a place to make their home.

The young male and female had just paired. They were two years old.

Later in winter, they would mate. The next spring, the female would have her first litter. The pair would raise their young together. They would probably stay together for life.

Earlier, the young male had left his family. He had searched for a mate. All along stream banks, he had made cone-shaped piles of mud. He mixed sticks and leaves into the mud.

The finished piles were 8 to 10 inches high. They were 10 to 12 inches across.

Then the male released a fluid from his anal glands onto the mud piles. The oily fluid was called *castoreum*. It had a sweet odor.

The female also had these scent glands. She, too, made mud piles to attract a mate. After a few days, the pair found each other. They began looking for a place to live. It had to be a good place to build a dam and a lodge. A *lodge* is the home or den of a beaver. Near the lodge, the beavers would make scented mud piles. These would mark their territory.

In the lodges these beavers had just left, new litters had been born. The new kits would spend about two years with their parents. Then they, too, would be on their own.

The male had traveled nearly four miles from the den where he had been born. The female had traveled about two miles.

The two beavers finally came to a small snow-water pond. They stopped to eat some skunk cabbage.

Beavers are vegetarians. In the spring, they eat roots, grasses, ferns, sedges, and other water plants. Later, they eat leaves, twigs, water lilies, fungi, duckweed, and berries. They also eat algae, which is rich in protein.

Beavers who live near farms eat crops. These include vegetables, fruits, wheat, and oats. And they love corn!

In the winter, beavers eat tree branches. They store the branches underwater near their dens.

Their favorite tree is the aspen. But they also like willow, poplar, birch, and maple.

Beavers store as much as they need for the winter months. They can eat up to two pounds of food a day.

A frog jumped into the water. The beavers paid no attention to it.

Overhead, a kingfisher flew back and forth over the stream. It swooped down suddenly. It caught a small fish in its long beak.

A pair of ducks bobbed in the water. They had a nest in the grass near the stream.

The beavers finished eating the skunk cabbage. They started back toward the stream. They were very nervous as they walked. Danger was greater when they were out of the water. They could not run very fast. So they would be no match against large predators.

The beavers continued up the stream. A deer came out of the woods. It was a doe. She drank from the stream. She had just had a fawn. The fawn was hidden in the tall grass in a grove of willows.

The beavers watched the deer. They stood very still. The female rubbed her nose against the male's nose. He sniffed her.

The doe bobbed her head up and down. She looked all around. Then she walked slowly back to where her fawn lay hidden.

The beavers decided they liked the area. Aspen, willow, and alder trees were all around. And the stream was not too swift here.

The beavers would rest awhile. Then they would build a dam.

CHAPTER

The beavers began to cut down trees. They stood on their hind legs and bit off chunks of wood.

Beavers' teeth are very sharp and strong. Their front teeth have a hard orange coating. This keeps the teeth from breaking or chipping.

Like all rodents, beavers' front teeth never stop growing. Gnawing on wood keeps them worn down to the right length.

Beavers have 20 teeth. The 4 front teeth are for biting chunks of wood. The 16 back teeth are for chewing. With one bite, beavers can chomp through a one-inch sapling. In 20 minutes, they can bring down a six-inch tree.

Beavers have flaps of skin behind their front teeth. One is on each side of their mouths. The flaps close together. Then the beavers don't swallow wood chips.

The female's tree was the first to fall. It was a four-inch aspen. She began to

chomp off the smaller branches.

A short time later, her mate's tree fell.

All that day and far into the night, the pair worked. They cut down trees. They pushed and pulled the tree trunks and branches into the stream.

The beavers laid them in a row across the stream. Then they added more and more branches and logs. They added rocks.

Finally, the pair plastered the open areas with mud. They carried the mud by holding it against their chests with their front paws.

Beavers seem to be born knowing how to make dams and build lodges. They do not have to be taught by their parents.

The main reason beavers build dams is for safety. They need protection because they are not fighters and cannot move fast. The deep water protects them from most animals.

After several days, the dam was completed. The beavers had sealed all the open places with mud. It was good and tight.

Now it was time to make the lodge.

The pond was filling with water. Only a small amount went over the dam. If the pond got too full, the beavers would make an opening in the dam. It would form a spillway to let out some of the water. This would keep the dam from breaking.

The pair of beavers began cutting limbs and logs for the lodge. For days, they pulled peeled logs and branches to the center of the pond. This is where they had decided to build their lodge.

First, they piled up logs, sticks, rocks, and mud on the bottom of the pond. The finished pile rose to about 6 feet above the surface of the pond. It was a little over 14 feet in diameter.

Then the beavers went underwater and made an opening in the center of the heap of logs and sticks. Above the water level, they cut out enough branches to make a chamber about 6 feet across and 2 feet high.

Then they made a second entrance. They would use this in case they needed to escape in a hurry. The openings had to be big enough to bring in small branches. They would eat those in the winter.

Finally, the lodge was finished. The beavers covered all of it but the top with mud. The open places on top were air vents. When the mud dried, it was like concrete.

Beavers are safe inside their tight lodges. Very few animals can break into beavers' lodges. This is especially true in the winter when they are frozen hard.

This cozy home would last the pair for years.

CHAPTER

Now that the dam and the lodge were built, the beavers could rest. They spent a lot of time eating and sleeping. They also groomed themselves. They cleaned and oiled their fur.

Beavers' coats are made up of guard hairs and underfur. Guard hairs protect the underfur. The underfur traps air. It holds air against beavers' skins. Air provides insulation. Even in icy cold water, beavers stay warm.

Beavers must keep their coats free of dirt. And they must keep them oiled.

Two small oil glands are found behind the beavers' scent glands near the base of their tails. Beavers rub this oil on their guard hairs to waterproof them.

Beavers' back feet are webbed. The front feet are not. At the end of each toe is a claw. The two middle toenails are split. Beavers use these split nails for combing their coats.

When they first come out of the water, beavers shake themselves hard. They rub their eyes. They smooth their whiskers. Then they comb their hair over and over. They finish their grooming by oiling their thick coats.

The male and female beavers weighed about 30 pounds each. They would gain a little more before winter.

Beavers are the largest rodents in North America. They are found in all states. The beaver is the state animal of Oregon.

Over the summer, many animals used the newly made pond. Deer came to drink every day. Frogs and fish swam in the pond. Turtles sunned themselves on the rocky shore. A pair of great blue herons caught small fish and water insects. At night, raccoons came looking for food.

One hot afternoon, a female black bear and her cub came to the pond. At the far end, the mother rolled over and over in the shallow water close to the shore.

The cub sat in the grass and watched. Then very slowly, he went into the water. But he only stayed for a short time.

From the other side of the pond, the beavers watched, wide-eyed. It was the first time they had seen bears.

Sometimes in the morning, the beavers stretched out on the bank to sunbathe. They only stayed in the sun a short time. If they stayed too long, their tails and feet dried out. So back into the water they would go.

CHAPTER 4

Summer ended. Leaves turned red and yellow. The nights grew colder.

Some of the birds left the area. They flew south. They would spend the winter there.

Winter would come soon. The beavers had to gather their food supply. They found enough tree branches and saplings to last until spring.

The beavers stored food underwater near the lodge. They had not cut down trees that still had sap in them. They would have spoiled in the water.

Day after day, the pair worked. The beavers wedged the limbs into the mud at the bottom of the pond. Storing food was hard work.

Native Americans have always respected beavers. The Crow Indians believed that after they died, they would come back as beavers. They called these hardworking, intelligent animals their brothers and sisters.

A Native American legend tells why the beaver has a flat tail.

In the beginning, Beaver had a long, fluffy, round tail.

One day, Beaver was gnawing down a tall birch tree. He gnawed and gnawed at the trunk of the tree.

At last, the tree began to fall. Beaver ran toward the pond. But he was not fast enough.

The huge tree fell on Beaver's furry tail. It pinned him fast. He pulled and tugged. But he could not get free.

After a long time, a young Indian came along. He was searching for a birch tree. The birch tree had to be just right to make a canoe.

When the Indian came to where Beaver lay pinned by the big tree, he stopped. This was it! He had found the perfect tree for his canoe.

The Indian rolled the tree off Beaver's tail. Beaver was so happy to be free. But his tail was a mess. The hair was gone. His tail was flat.

To this day, Beaver's tail is flat and hairless. And he has still never learned to bring down a tree exactly where he wants it.

At last, the beavers' work was finished. Snow fell. Some days, the temperature fell below freezing. But inside the lodge, the pair was snug and warm.

In February, the pair mated. The female would carry her young for three and a half months.

During the winter, the beavers left the den only to get food. They would swim

to their food supply and select a branch.

Back at the lodge, the beavers pulled the branch through the opening. Then they chewed the branch into pieces about one foot long. To eat, the beavers stood on their hind legs. They held the pieces between their front paws and chewed the bark off the way people eat ears of corn.

The bare sticks were taken out of the den and left in the water. Later, they could be used to repair the dam.

Finally, it was May. It was almost time for the female to have her babies. But first, she made a nest.

Some animals make nests of soft grasses and leaves. But beavers don't. Grasses and leaves would mold underwater.

The female made her nest of wood. She split the pieces of wood into long fibers. They were very thin and soft.

When the female began her labor, the male left the lodge. He would stay away about two weeks. Then he would return and help raise the babies.

Three days later, the female gave birth to three kits. Gus was the first born. He was the only male. The kits weighed nearly a pound each. They were almost 14 inches long.

Gus and his sisters were born with fur. Their eyes were open, and they had teeth.

The mother cleaned her babies. They squirmed and whined like puppies. When the mother finished cleaning them, each kit latched on to a nipple. They nursed noisily.

Gus was warm and happy. He nestled between his sisters. It was dark inside the lodge.

Gus could not see too well. But he could smell and hear. He liked the smell of his home. It smelled of wood and water. And he liked the smell of his mother and sisters too.

He liked the sounds. He heard the water lapping against the lodge floor and the wind blowing outside the den. He especially liked the sounds his mother made. These were soft humming sounds. They seemed to say, "Nothing will harm you. Mother is here."

Gus would answer with his own humming sounds. It was good to be a baby beaver and have a warm snug home. It was good to have a mother to feed and care for him. And it was good to have sisters to play with. Gus was happy and comfortable.

By the time Gus was five days old, he could paddle in the small pool in the center of the lodge. He loved the feel of water. He could put his head underwater. And he could still see.

Beavers have transparent eyelids. These cover the eyes when they are underwater.

Beavers' ears and nostrils have valves that close when they swim. Then water can't enter.

Beavers have lungs that hold a lot of oxygen—more than human lungs. They can stay underwater for 15 minutes.

Their webbed back feet are made for swimming. Their front feet are not

webbed. When they swim, they make fists with their front feet. They hold them against their chests.

Gus's father finally returned. He sniffed his new babies. Gus sniffed his father. It was a good smell. It was almost the same as his mother's.

Now the three kits had two parents to care for them. They were doubly safe.

Besides nursing, Gus's favorite thing to do was wrestle with his sisters. How they squealed and chirped as they tumbled about in the nest!

CHAPTER

Gus was going swimming in the big pond outside the lodge! Finally, he was going out to see the big world.

It was early dusk. Gus's father left the lodge first. He looked all around. He made a circle around the lodge. Everything seemed okay. It was safe to bring out his family.

Gus's mother came out. She was followed by the three kits. Gus was in the lead.

The kits were a little over two weeks old. They had more than doubled their weight.

Gus began to paddle. His sisters began to paddle. Gus swam around his father. His little hind feet moved fast in the water.

One of Gus's sisters got tired. Her mother swam under her. The female baby rode on her mother's back. What fun!

Gus decided he would like that. He swam to his mother. He grabbed her fur with his front feet. He pulled himself onto her back. He settled down next to his sister.

The father beaver made a whistling sound. The other sister swam to him. She was very tired. She climbed on her father's back.

This was the first time the family had swum in the big pond. So they did not go far from the lodge.

Gus slipped back into the water. He paddled behind his mother.

Something else was paddling on the water. It wasn't too far from the beaver family. Gus stared at it. What was it? It wasn't a beaver. It didn't look like him or his sisters.

Suddenly, it made a loud sound. QUACK! QUACK! Then it flew off through the air.

The kits were very tired when they returned to the lodge. The mother groomed her three babies. Then she groomed herself. Their father groomed himself.

Gus and his sisters nibbled on some tender twigs. They were sweet and juicy.

Then the kits snuggled close to their mother and nursed hungrily. How good the warm milk tasted. Gus and his sisters fell asleep. They were all worn out after their first big swimming lesson.

Every day, the kits went swimming with their parents. They grew stronger day by day.

Gus climbed onto a big log. His sisters climbed on too. The sun was warm. It felt good.

The mother beaver swam around the log. She nibbled on a water plant.

Suddenly, a dark shadow appeared above. Down it swooped. The mother beaver slapped the water hard with her big, flat tail. *Whop!* That meant danger!

The kits jumped into the water. They just missed being a hawk's dinner.

Dangers seemed to be everywhere while the kits were young. Not too many animals bother grown beavers. But kits can be caught by owls, hawks, otters,

and even large fish. Mother and father beavers must keep a constant eye on their young. Beavers are very good parents.

At six weeks, Gus and his sisters were weaned. They ate all kinds of food now. But they did not eat meat. Like all beavers, the kits were strictly vegetarians.

CHAPTER 6

Gus's first summer was fun. He played with his sisters and his parents. He had all he wanted to eat and a comfortable, safe place to live.

By the time he was a few months old, Gus had seen most of the other animals in the area. He knew which ones were dangerous.

When he heard coyotes or wolves howl, Gus kept very still. He listened. They were sounds he did not like.

When a large bird flew overhead, he dived into the water.

Once, Gus saw a bear walk around the pond. But that did not scare him. It was far away.

Another time, Gus was swimming in deep water. He was near the shore. He had just picked water plants from the bottom of the pond.

Gus came to the top of the pond with the plants. Suddenly, he was face-to-face with a gigantic monster. The monster was standing knee-deep in the water. Its mouth was full of dripping grass.

Gus let out a shriek. He slapped the water with the flat of his tail. He swam to the lodge as fast as his webbed feet would paddle.

 44

He had no way of knowing that the
monster was a moose. And it wasn't the
least bit interested in a beaver.

Fall came. It was time to repair the dam.
The beavers had to make sure it was tight.
They checked the spillways. They had to
be just right or the dam would break.

Gus and his sisters helped with the repair work. They carried mud. They filled in the open spaces. They gathered sticks for plugging holes.

After the sap went down in the trees, the beavers gnawed them down. They stored branches underwater. They carried rocks to hold them down in the mud at the bottom of the pond.

All around the pond and in the forest, animals were ready for winter. The squirrels and chipmunks had stored nuts.

They would hole up through the winter. Bears were hibernating in dens and hollow logs. Some water animals had burrowed into the mud. Many birds had flown south.

And inside the lodge, the beaver family was snug and warm. On cold days, the vapor from their warm bodies and breath rose through the air vents of their den. It looked like smoke coming out of a chimney.

The beavers didn't mind the winter. But spring was welcome.

Now Gus and his family spent more time outside the lodge. After a diet of only twigs and bark, spring was a good time. New green plants were growing.

The mother beaver was about to give birth again. Gus, his sisters, and father left the lodge. For about two weeks, they lived in burrows in the bank of the pond.

When they returned, Gus and his sisters had four new siblings—two sisters and two brothers. The lodge was crowded. But there was still room for everyone.

Gus was a year old. He weighed about 18 pounds.

An adult beaver can weigh up to 60 pounds. Prehistoric beavers were very large. These giant beavers lived a million years ago. They weighed about 750 pounds. Skeletons have been found in Indiana.

In 1921, a beaver was killed that weighed 100 pounds. In 1938, someone killed one that weighed 115 pounds. But this is rare.

There have been a few cases of people keeping beavers as pets. But they are difficult pets to care for. You would need your own pond and lots and lots of trees.

Some years ago, a woman in New York started a *haven*, or safe home, for beavers. The haven covered about 1,300 acres. A stream ran through the land. The beavers turned it into a pond.

Thousands of people came to the haven to see the beavers. The woman made pets of some of them. One even lived in an addition on her house.

But usually it is not a good idea to make pets of wild animals.

Like most animals, Gus grew up and left home. He was two years old. His sisters left home at the same time.

Gus moved a long way from the den. He found a mate. They built a dam and a lodge together. If Gus and his mate were lucky, they could live at least ten years. And they would raise lots and lots of little beavers.

Many changes would take place over the years. The beavers would move on when there was no more food. The dam would break. The water would flow away. Only the bare mud bottom with a small stream running through would remain.

In time, cattails and other plants would grow along the edge of the pond. Blackbirds would nest there.

In time, grass and plants would begin to grow where trees once stood. It would become a meadow.

Many, many years later, seeds from trees would start to spring up. Finally, it would once more become a forest.

▲ ▼ ▲ ▼ ▲ ▼ ▲ ▼ ▲

FOR MORE INFORMATION, CONTACT
Beavers: Wetlands and Wildlife
146 Van Dyke Rd.
Dolgesville, NY 13329
Web site: www.beaversww.org